Silly Tricks

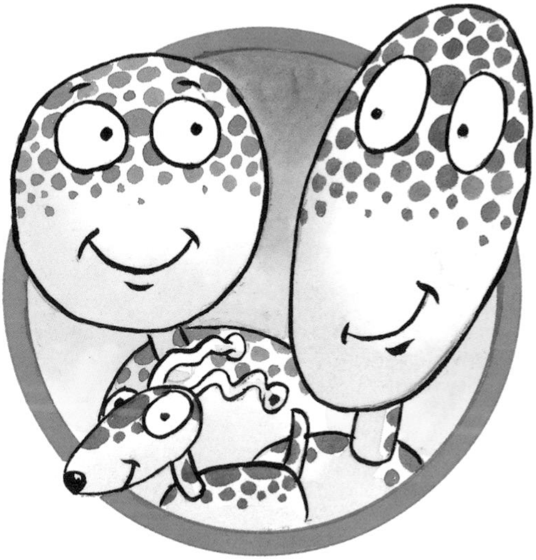

Illustrated by Dave Gunson

Rigby

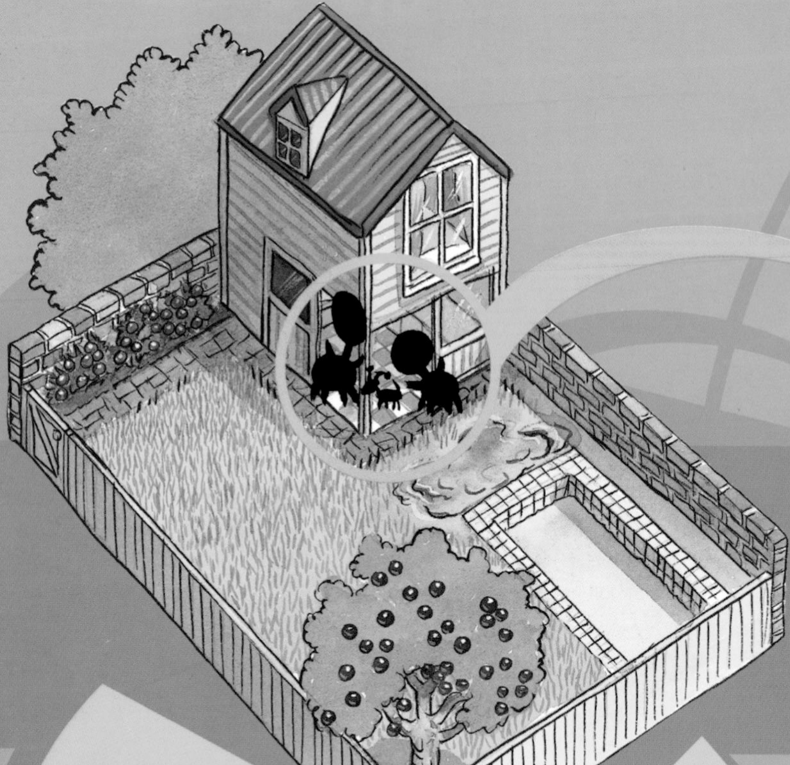

We are
in the house.

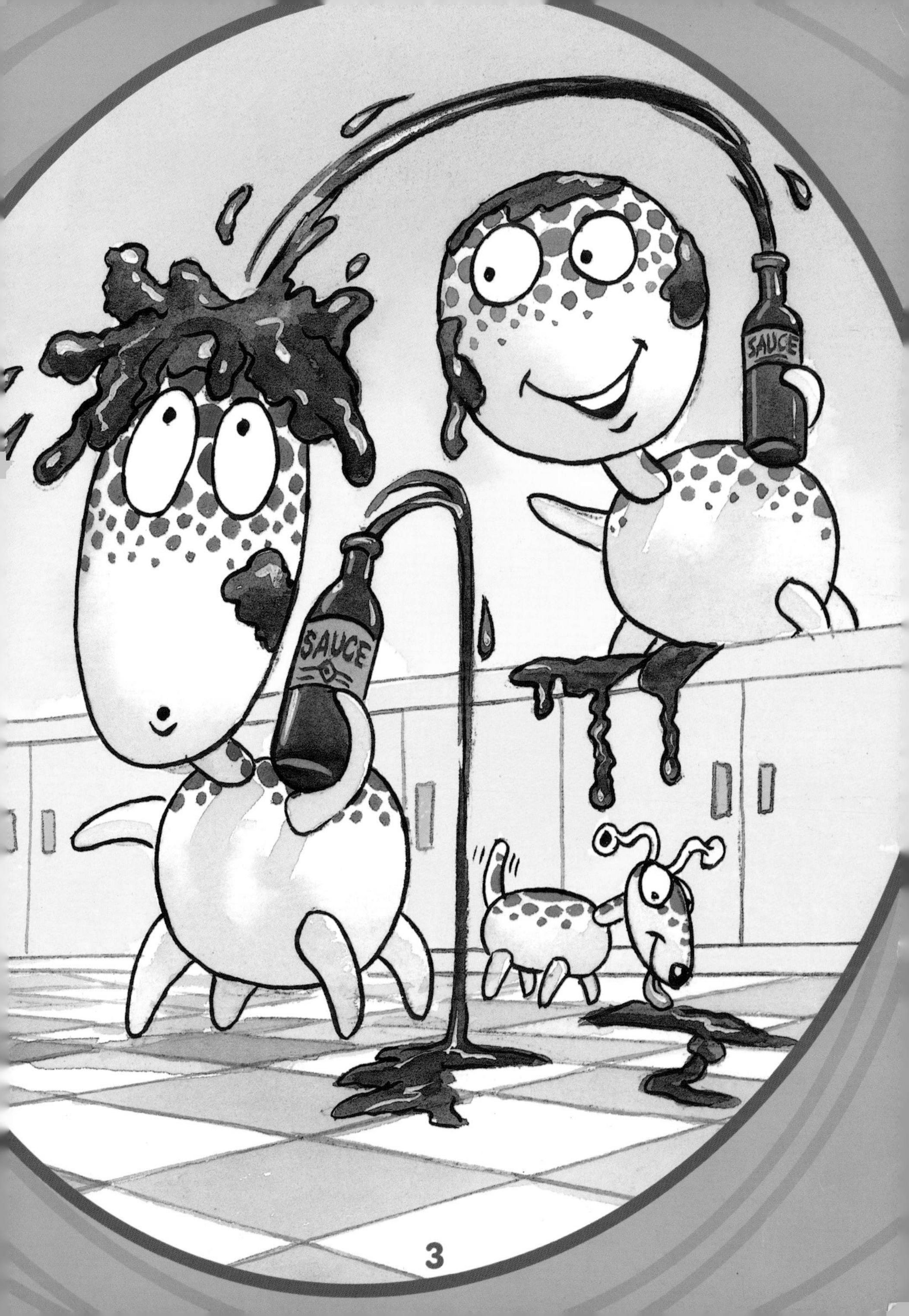
SAUCE
SAUCE

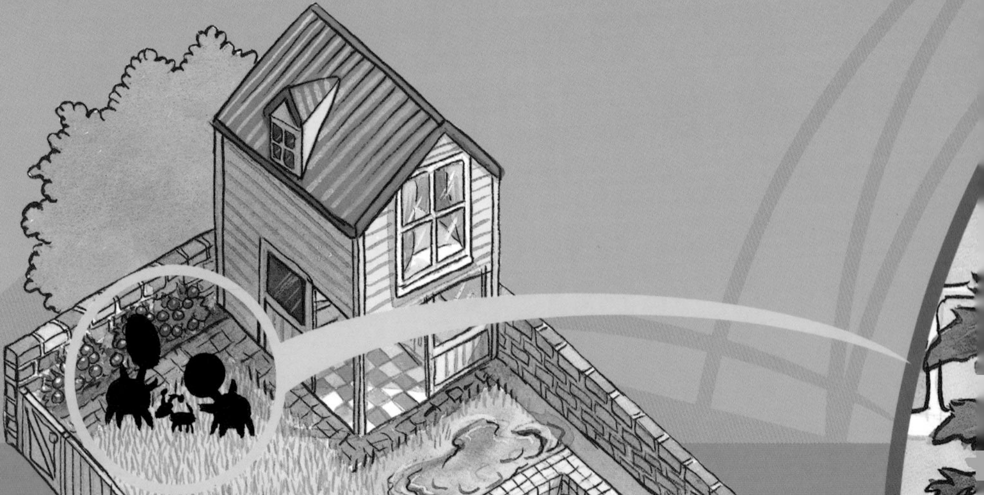

We are
in the garden.

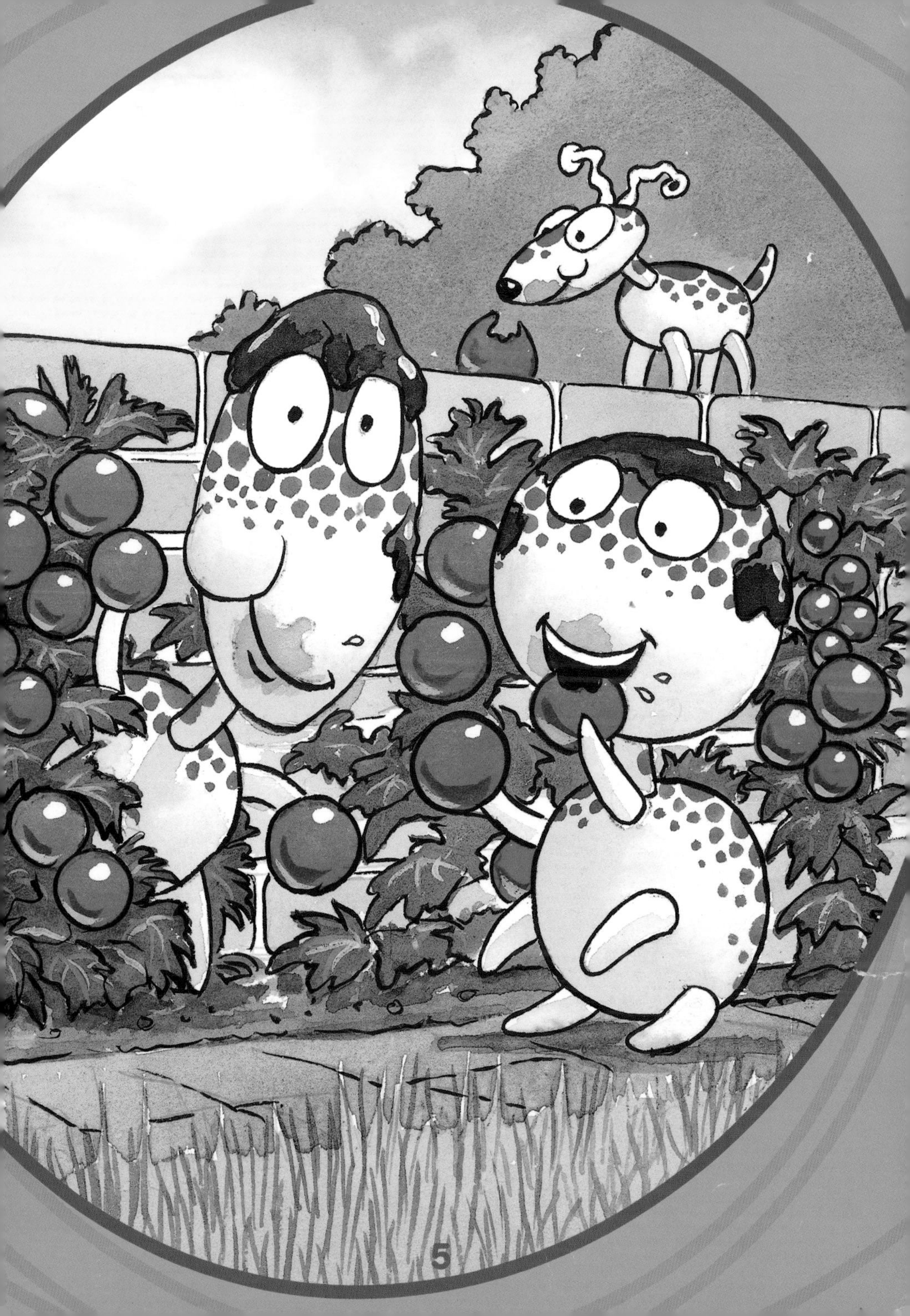

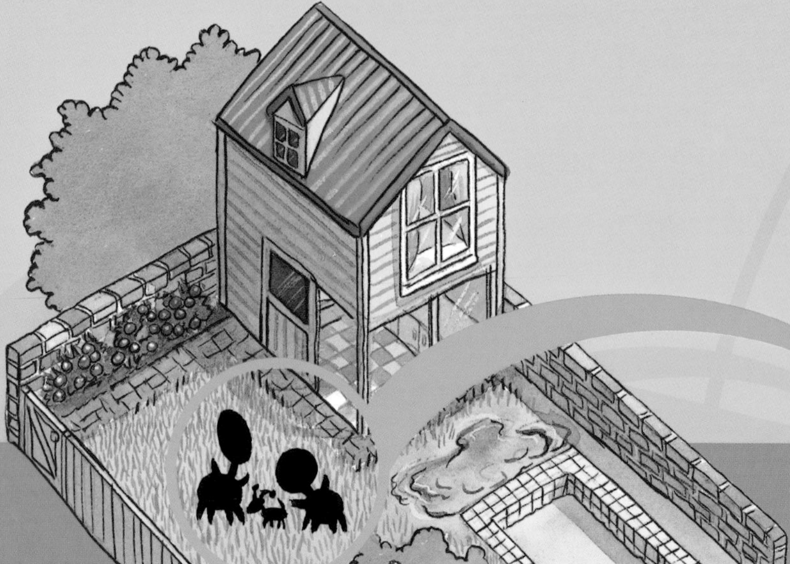

We are
in the grass.

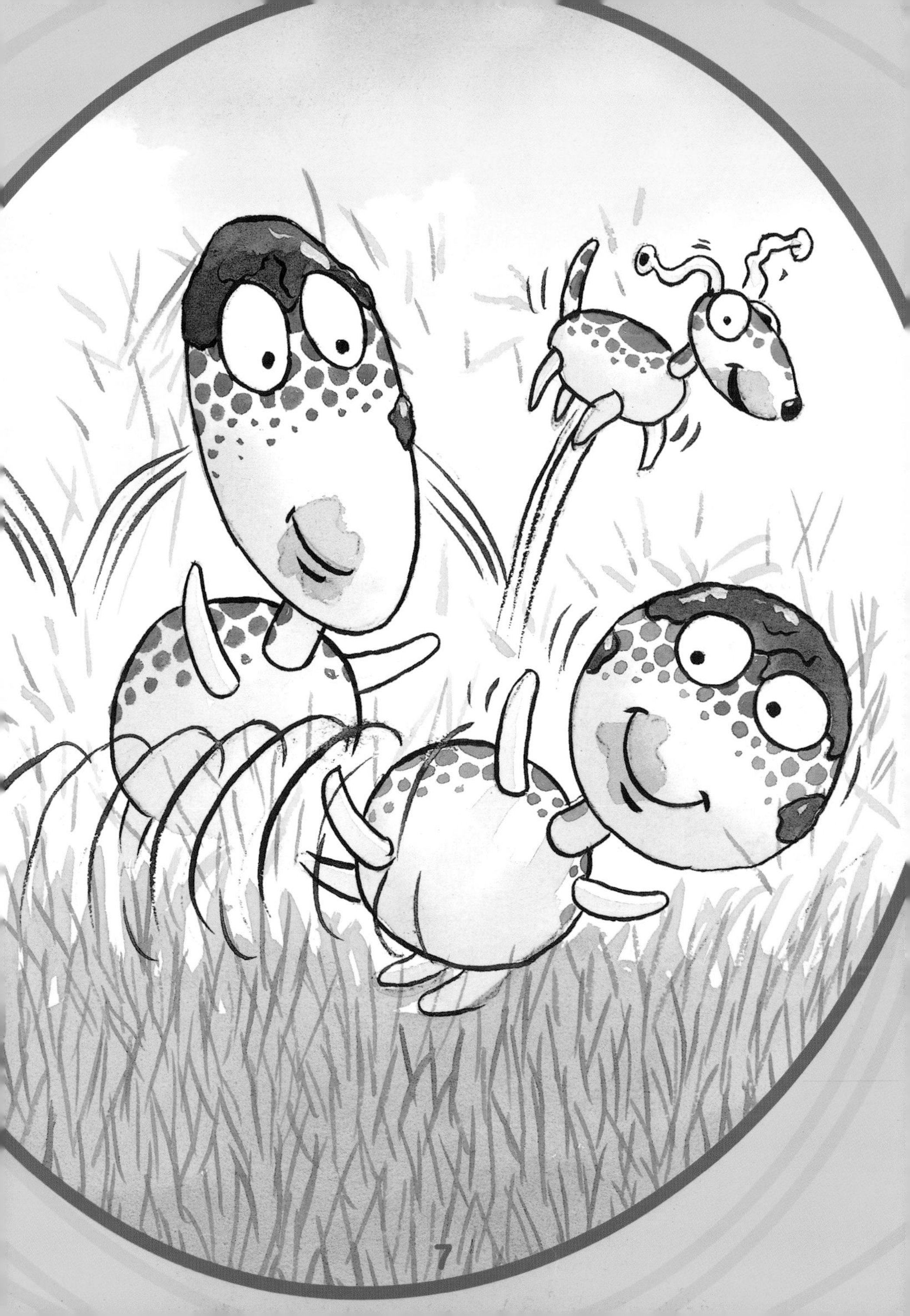

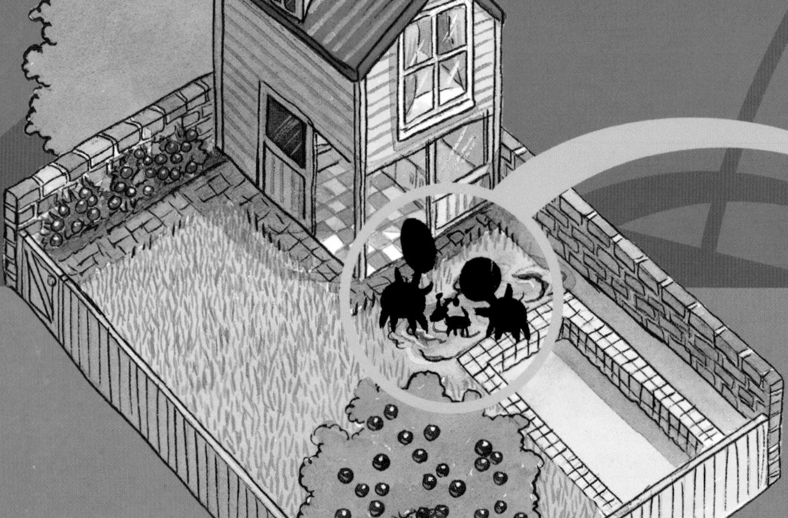

We are
in the mud.

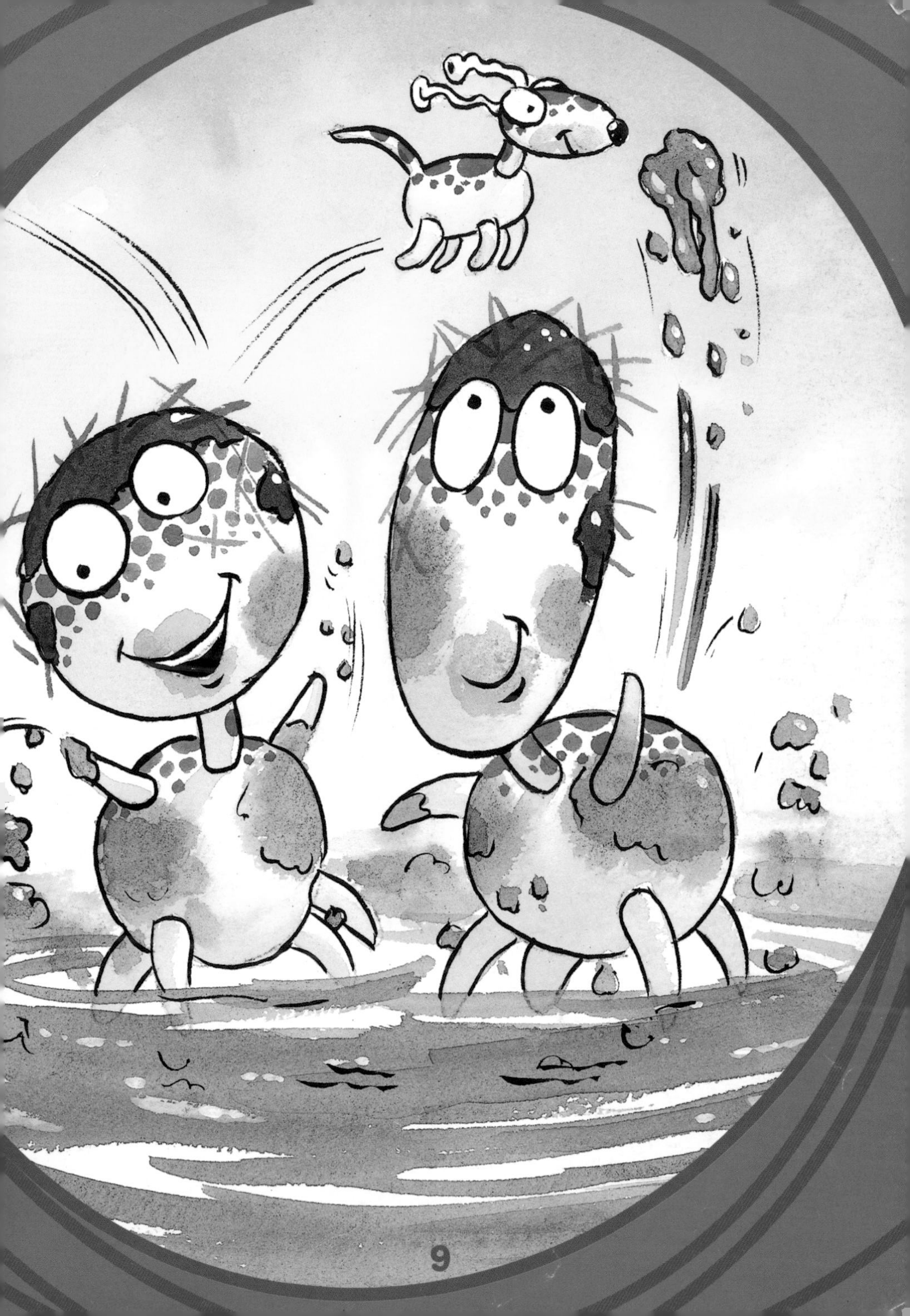

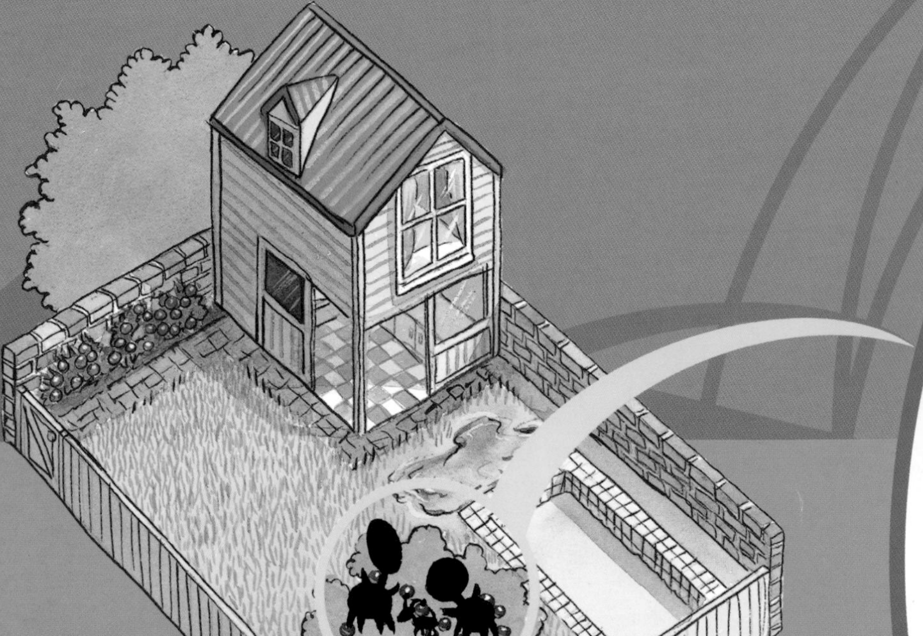

We are
in the tree.

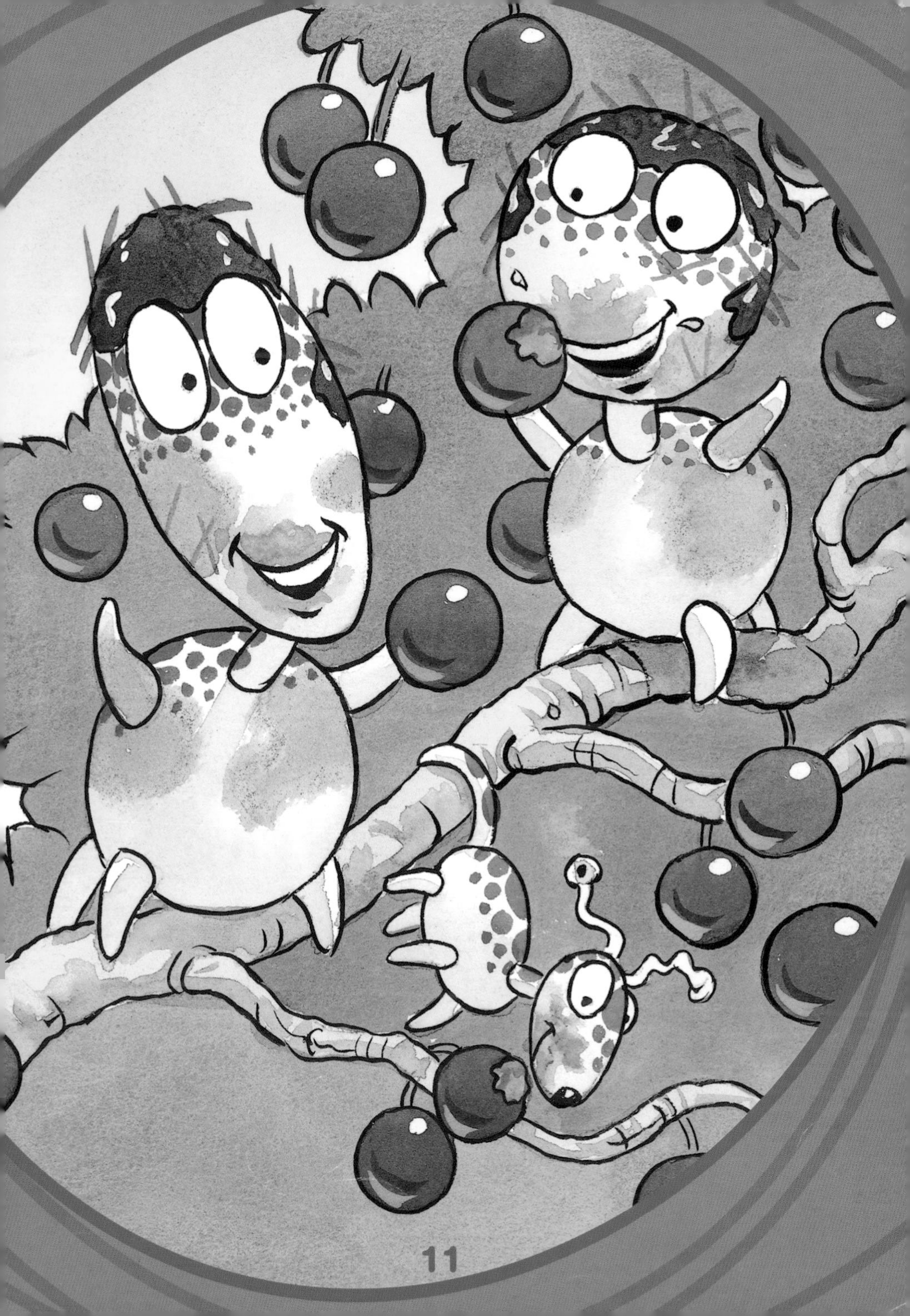

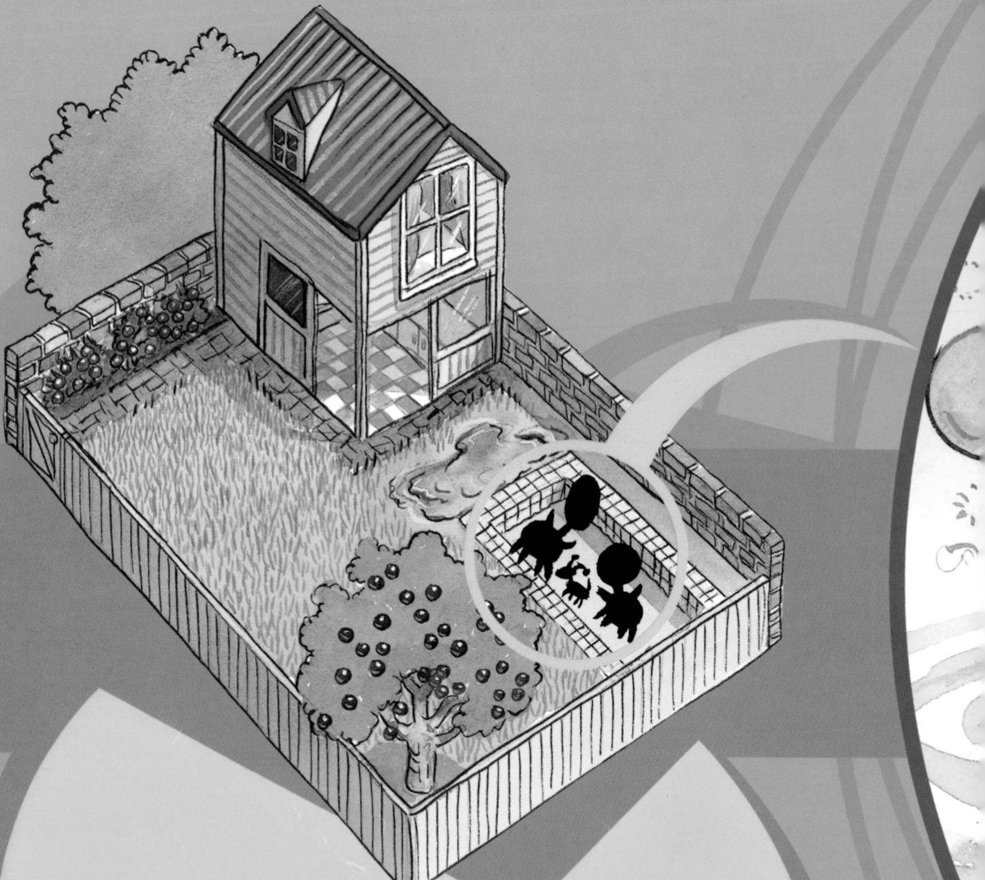

We are
in the pool.

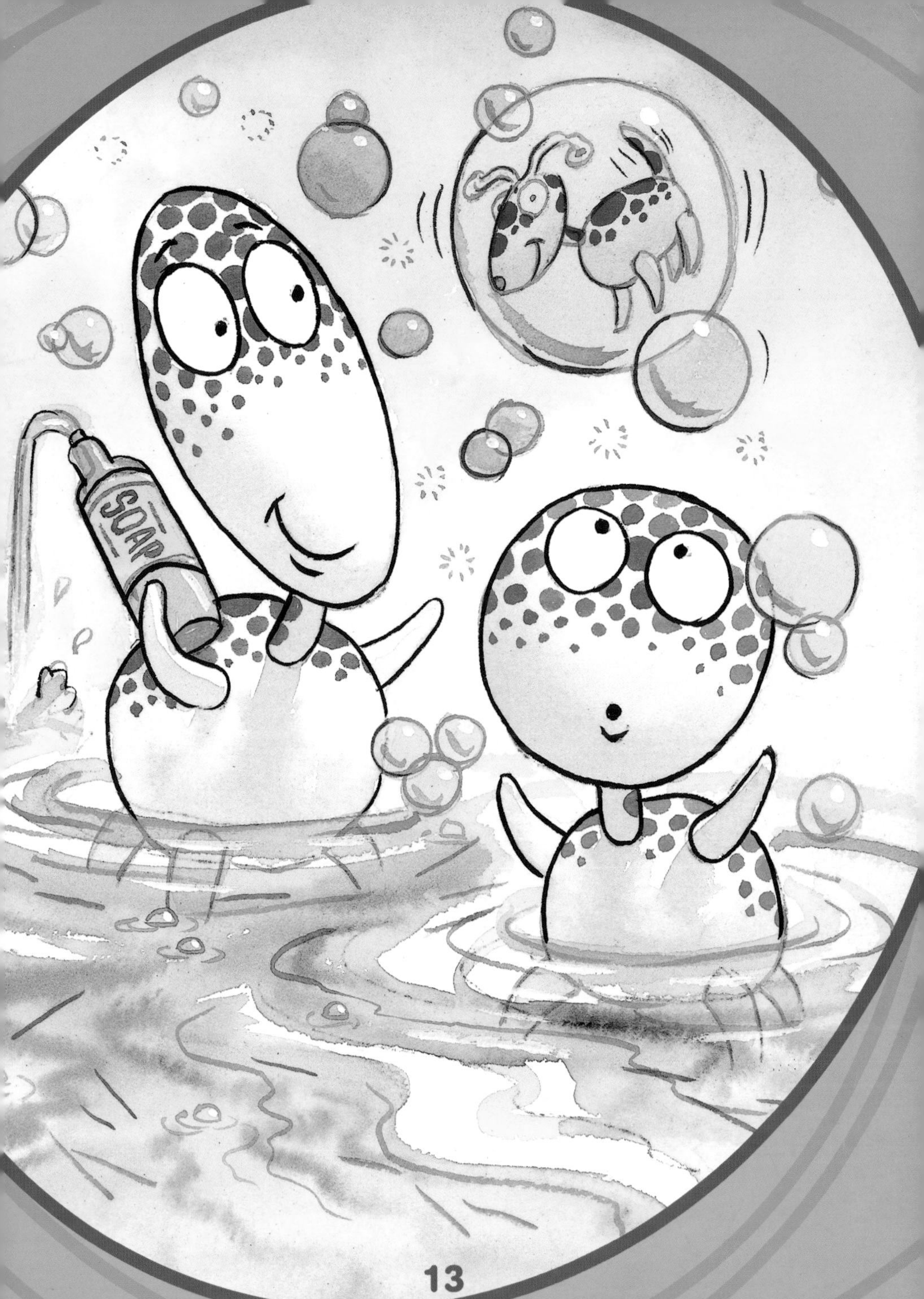
SOAP

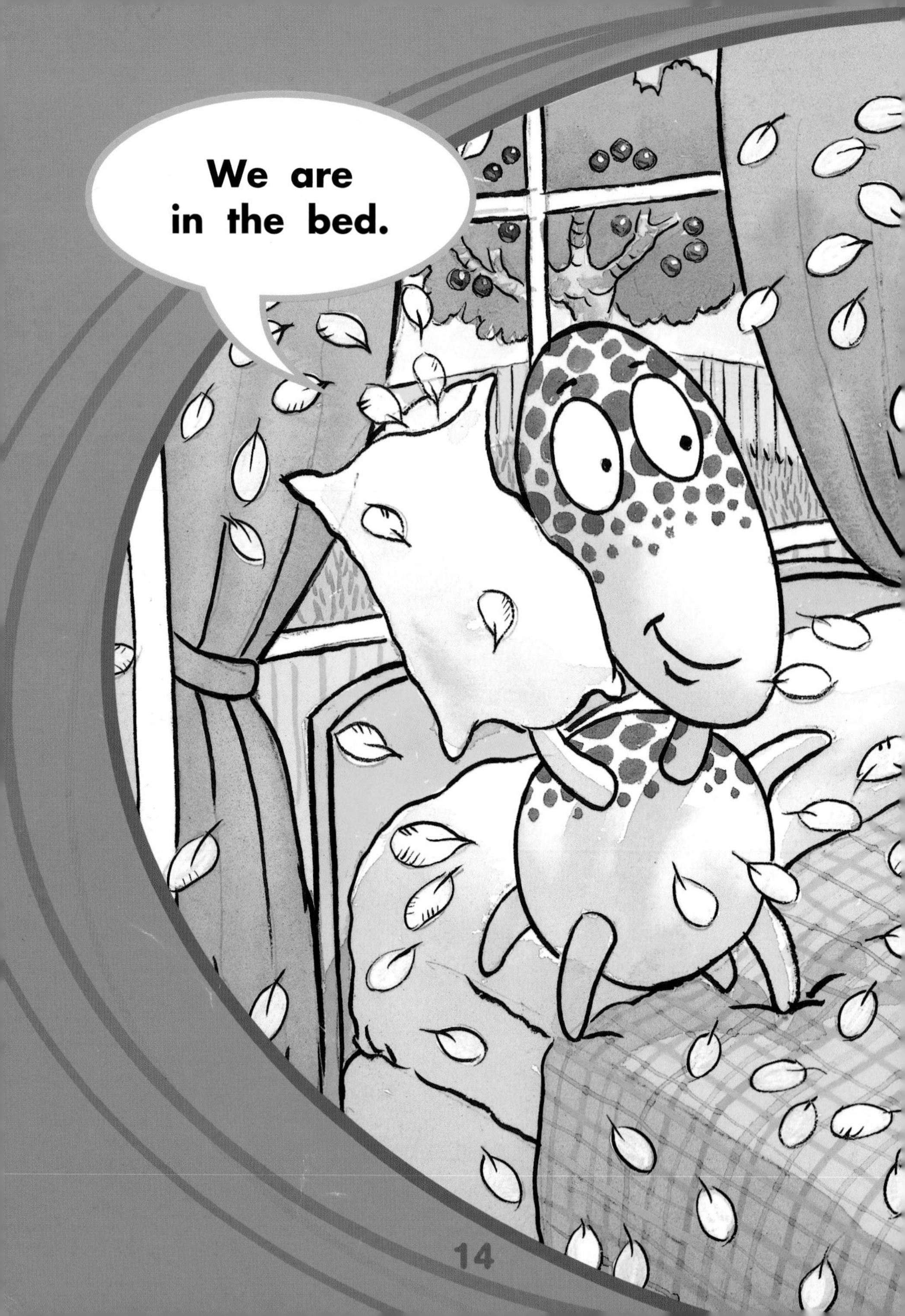
We are in the bed.

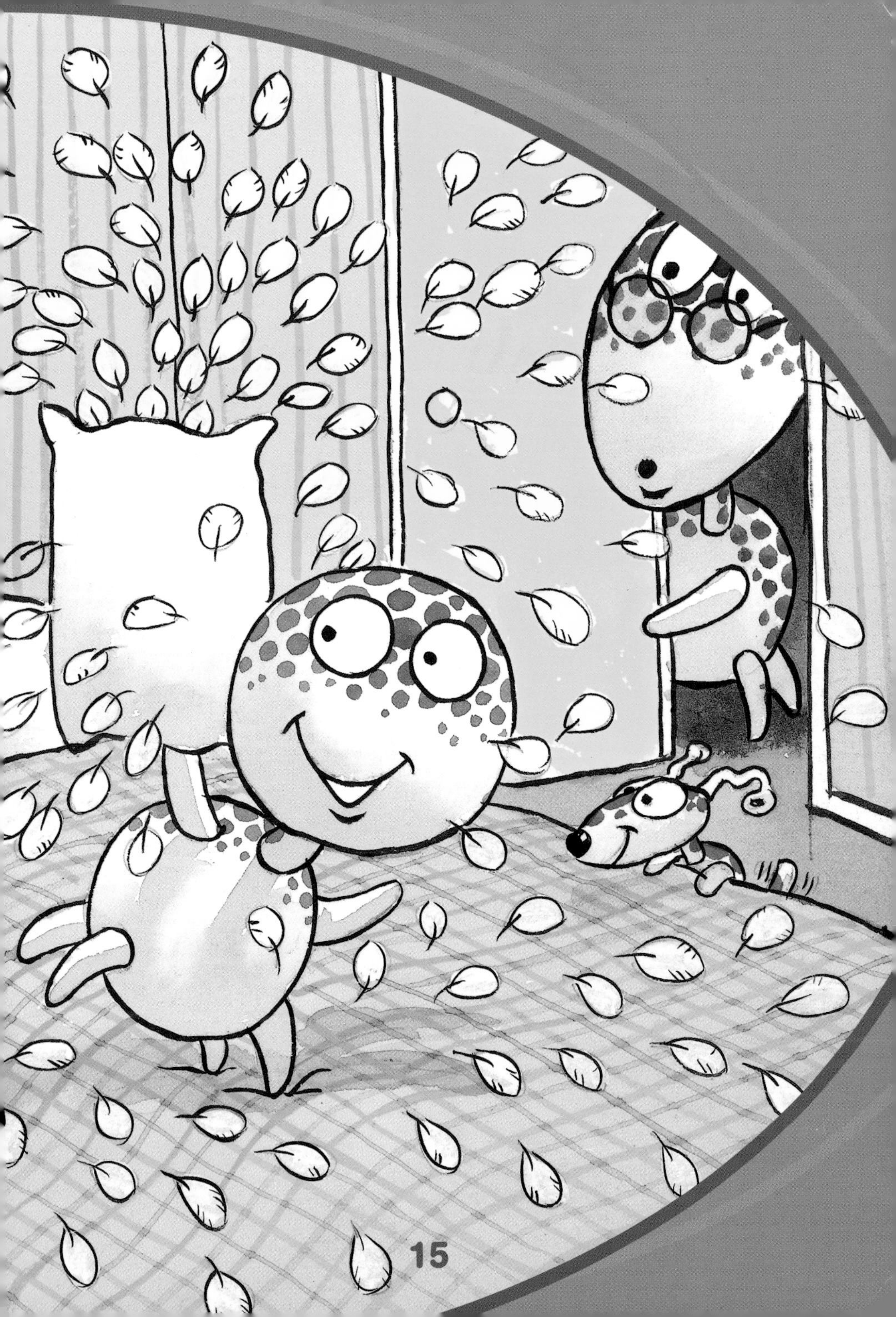

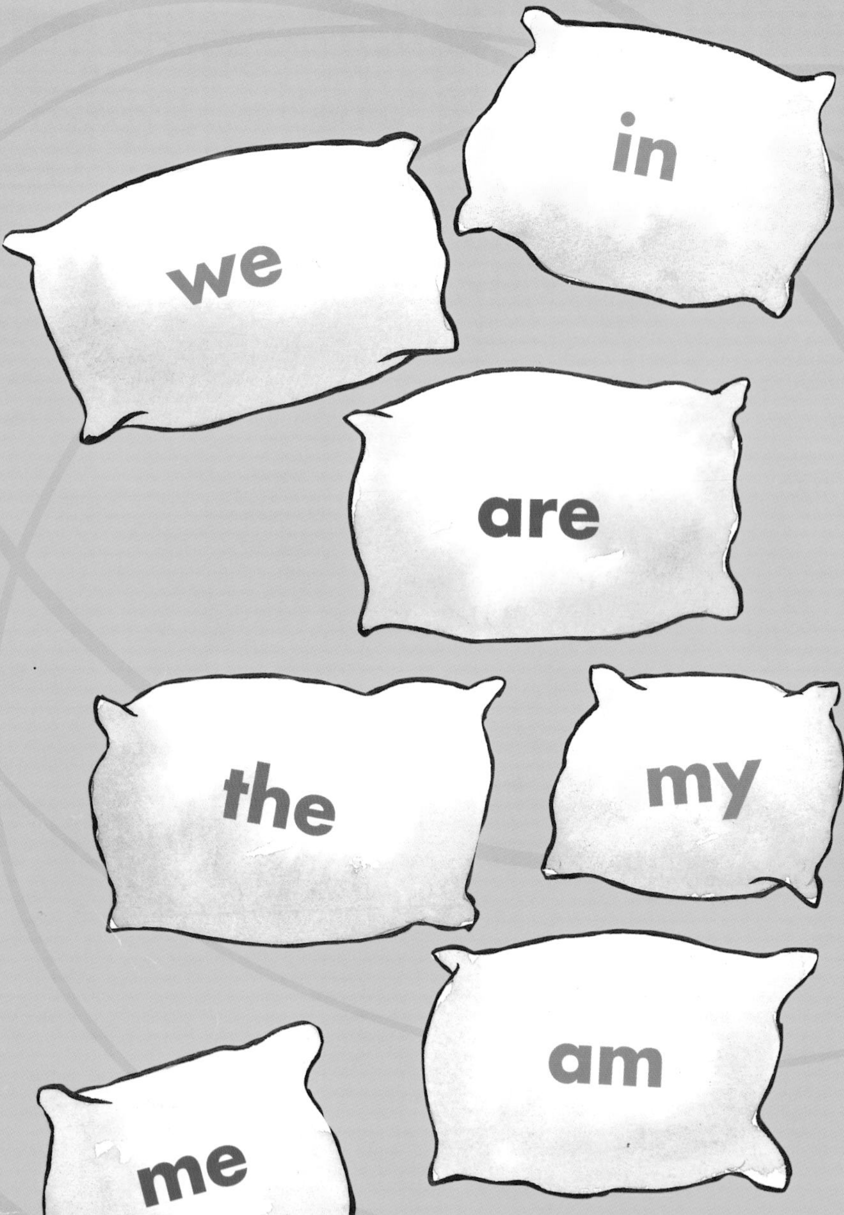
in
we
are
the
my
am
me